MOLASSES MAN

by **Kathy L. May**

illustrated by
Felicia Marshall

HOLIDAY HOUSE / New York

The author thanks David Jones
and the Madison County molasses makers

Text copyright © 2000 by Kathy L. May
Illustrations copyright © 2000 by Felicia Marshall
All Rights Reserved
Printed in the United States of America
www.holidayhouse.com
First Edition
The text typeface is Goudy Old Style.

Library of Congress Cataloging-in-Publication Data
May, Kathy.
Molasses man / by Kathy L. May; illustrated by Felicia Marshall.—1st ed.
p.   cm.
Summary: A young boy describes how he watches his grandfather
as all the family works together to harvest the sorghum cane and make molasses.
ISBN 0-8234-1438-8
[1. Molasses—Fiction. 2. Grandfathers—Fiction.
3. Afro-Americans—Fiction.] I. Marshall, Felicia, ill.   II. Title.
PZ7.M4526 Mo 2000
[E]—dc21   98-021223

For Garry

With special thanks to Mr. Louis Farmer,
the real "Molasses Man"

K. L. M.

I jump off the school bus one warm afternoon in September, and Grandpa's waiting for me on the front porch.

"Let's go check the cane," he says.

We put on our boots and walk out to the fields. Our patch of sorghum cane is tall and green and leafy, like corn. Grandpa plucks some seeds off the top of a plant. He drops the hard red seeds into my hands. He says we'll make molasses tomorrow.

Early the next morning, after breakfast, all of us except Grandpa work in the sorghum patch. My cousins and I go down the rows of plants, stripping off the long green leaves. My mama and big sisters follow, cutting off the seed heads.

Next come Papa and my uncles. They chop the cane stalks off at the ground with long knives. My cousin Danny and I have a pretend sword fight with two of the stalks.

We stack the stalks on the flatbed, and then we all ride back to the house, where Grandpa is waiting on the porch.

While Papa and my uncles unload the cane
into the yard, I help Grandpa carry his molasses-
making tools and big cooker pan out of the shed,
where they've been stored for a whole year now.

The cooker pan is a long metal box, like a
shallow bathtub. We set it on the ground and fill it
with soapy water to wash the cans and buckets and
ladles and skimmers. Then we scrub and rinse the
cooker itself. We lift the cooker onto the stone
furnace Grandpa built in the yard.

Uncle Lester begins splitting firewood. I gather sticks and fallen branches from the ground for kindling. Then Uncle Lester loads up the furnace.

Grandpa bends down with a box of matches and gets the fire going. He pokes the sticks and tends the fire until it's burning steady but not too hot.

Papa and my uncle Jim haul out the juicer engine. They feed the raw green stalks into the rollers. The juicer is as loud as a lawnmower, and for a few minutes we can't hear each other talk. Then the juice flows out watery and yellowish green, like limeade, into a barrel.

Papa and Uncle Jim pour buckets of juice into the cooker pan. I carry Grandpa's slat-back chair down from the porch to the furnace, where he sits nearby to keep watch.

Pretty soon the juice begins to boil with tiny foamy bubbles. It smells strong and sour. Grandma comes down from the house with a thermos of coffee for the grown-ups and a jug of water for us kids.

Grandpa says when he was a boy they used mule power to grind the cane. They hitched a mule to the end of a long wooden pole, and that mule would walk around and around in circles, pulling the pole that turned the rollers and squeezed the juice out of the cane.

Mama and I take turns with my sisters and aunts, standing at the cooker pan with flat wooden skimmers. We skim the yellow froth off the top and scrape it into buckets. It's steamy hot standing over the cooker pan, but it feels good on this chilly morning. We dip and skim and scrape, laughing and singing and talking.

After lunch I give my skimmer to a neighbor who drops by to help. Then I play freeze tag and hide-and-seek with my cousins in the yard. But I don't stay away from the molasses for long.

I like to stand by Grandpa's chair at the end of the pan where big slow bubbles rise to the surface. Frog's eyes, Grandpa calls them. Every now and then he stirs the molasses, lifts his ladle, and lets the syrup slide down in long strings. He can tell just by looking when it's cooked enough. Grandpa never lets the sweetness boil away.

When Grandpa declares the molasses done, he turns the knob on the cooker pan to let it flow out. The molasses goes through a strainer into a big metal can. It's darker than honey, brown as the earth, brown as my skin.

While some molasses is cooling for us in a bowl, one of the kids goes up to the house for spoons. Then we all dip spoons into the bowl for a taste, and everybody is smiling and praising Grandpa.

Late in the afternoon when the molasses in the can has cooled enough, Mama and my aunts pour it into glass jars. They put lids on the jars and carry them to the table they've set up near the road.

Everybody comes from miles around to buy my Grandpa's
molasses. Friends and neighbors and even strangers passing
through take jars of our molasses home to spread on their biscuits
or to put in cakes or cookies or gingerbread.

Lots of people who don't know Grandpa's name just call him "Molasses Man." He says he doesn't mind. He can't remember all their names, either.

They walk up to him real slow and hesitant, like they don't want to bother him. When he turns around, they tell him they sure do like his molasses. Then he shakes their hands.

Grandpa says I'm going to be in charge one day. My mama and aunts are too busy running up to the house and tending to the stand. My papa and uncles have their own work to do.

Grandpa hands me the wooden ladle and motions for me to use it. He says I've got an eye for making molasses. I say I've got a taste for it, too, and we laugh.

Author's Note

In many rural areas of the United States, especially in the South, sorghum has been planted and harvested for making molasses for well over two hundred years. Sorghum molasses provided sweetening for cooking and baking and was often used when white cane sugar was scarce. Before modern food-processing factories and grocery stores, most everyone in the rural South grew a patch of sorghum.

Usually there would be one special person in a community who had the skills and the tools to be the "molasses man." After harvesting the plants in the fall, people would take their sorghum cane to the home of the molasses maker or he would go to someone's house and they'd have a molasses "stir-off" with a dozen or more families participating. This would be an all-day event that combined work and play. A stir-off would usually include, along with the work of making the molasses, a big meal, lots of conversation and socializing, fun and games, and often the music from a fiddle or banjo. Guests would stay until late at night and then go home with a gallon or two of warm molasses. The molasses maker would receive a large portion of the molasses as pay.

Nowadays it is becoming rare for any farm family to make molasses. But once in a while, if you drive on the back roads, you can find a stand where someone is selling jars of homemade molasses and, if you're lucky, a large cooker pan or evaporator where the molasses is just coming to a slow boil. Whether you buy it from a country roadside stand or in a grocery store, molasses is still great for baking cookies and gingerbread.